W9-BSJ-386

Mr. Karp's Last Glass

Mr. Karp's Last Glass

CARY FAGAN

PICTURES BY *Selçuk Demirel*

GROUNDWOOD BOOKS
HOUSE OF ANANSI PRESS
TORONTO BERKELEY

Published in Canada and the USA in 2008 by Groundwood Books

Groundwood Books / House of Anansi Press
110 Spadina Avenue, Suite 801, Toronto, Ontario M5V 2K4
or c/o Publishers Group West
1700 Fourth Street, Berkeley, CA 94710

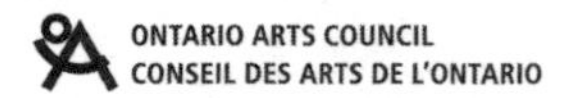

We acknowledge for their financial support of our publishing program the Canada Council for the Arts, the Government of Canada through the Book Publishing Industry Development Program (BPIDP) and the Ontario Arts Council.

Library and Archives Canada Cataloguing in Publication
Fagan, Cary
Mr. Karp's last glass / Cary Fagan ; illustrated by Selçuk Demirel.
ISBN-13: 978-0-88899-790-6 (bound).–ISBN-10: 0-88899-790-6 (bound)
ISBN-13: 978-0-88899-835-4 (pbk.)–ISBN-10: 0-88899-835-X (pbk.)
I. Demirel, Selçuk II. Title.
PS8561.A375M58 2008 jC813'.54 C2007-906089-7

Design by Michael Solomon
Printed and bound in Canada

For Rebecca,
with all my heart

~ 1 ~

My Father the Thief

A LOT OF KIDS collect things. Baseball cards. Comics. Beanie Babies. Whenever I went over to a friend's house or to visit one of my girl cousins, and they showed me their collections of Popsicle sticks thrown into a box or little glass animals on a shelf, I pretended to be interested. But the truth is, all I could think was how boring, how *unoriginal* they all were.

They weren't serious collectors. Not like me.

I started young. Stones when I was four years old. Snowglobes when I was six. Shoe horns when I was eight.

Now, at the age of eleven, I had three collections: beer-bottle caps, writing instruments and words.

I had fifty-six beer-bottle caps, each one from a different kind of beer. One was from Musker Beer, made in our own town, but I also had a Grolsch cap (Holland), a Keith's (Nova Scotia), and even one from India. Some I got by asking in restaurants, but we didn't go to restaurants very often. Some I found in parks or at the beach, and some I got from my dad. My dad was willing to buy a different kind of beer each time he went to the store, but beer came in cartons of six or twelve, and he only drank one on Friday night and one on Saturday, and my mom preferred wine, so my collection wasn't growing very fast.

I kept the caps in a series of cigar boxes, each divided into little sections with cardboard and tape, one spot for each cap.

In my writing instruments collection, which was the newest, I had twenty-three different pens — everything from an old steel-nibbed fountain pen that had belonged to my grandfather on my mom's side, to an astronaut pen that could write upside down, to a pen so tiny you had to hold it with the tips of your fingers. (The ink had already run out in that one.)

I suppose my word collection was a bit different, as I didn't "own" them in the usual sense. I was given the two-volume Oxford English Dictionary for my birthday this year. That's the one with such small print that it comes with a magnifying glass. Whenever I heard a word that I didn't know, I would look it up. Beside the definition I would place a little check mark with my pencil. Each word that I checked off became part of my word collection.

Otherwise, I was a pretty regular kid. I would have watched television ten hours a day if my parents had let me, and I liked playing baseball and video games and eating just about anything that was bad for me. But I thought of myself as a serious and interesting collector.

That is, until I met Mr. Karp.

Mr. Karp moved in because my father

lost his job. My dad worked as the hardware section manager of a LoPri Store, a job he'd had for almost six years before he was accused of stealing and was fired.

You might not know LoPri stores unless you live in a small or medium-sized town — a place too small for the giant chains like Wal-Mart and Costco. LoPri employees, including my father, had to wear fake straw hats ("boaters" my dad said they were called), purple aprons and striped bowties. They had to greet customers with a cheerful "Good morning, are you here to save?" no matter what mood they were in. And they had to keep the high pyramids of products like duct tape and hairdryers neat and orderly because the customers were always messing them up.

My father was accused of stealing a metal gardening shed, a DVD collection of *I Love Lucy* television shows, a Barbie camper van, five bags of red licorice, a pink imitation Christmas tree with musical angel, a coffee-bean grinder, a Sidney Crosby hockey stick, a pair of steel-toed workboots and a five-string banjo with instruction manual.

One morning, three men from head office came to the store and, in front of all the people my father worked with, asked him to hand over his fake boater, his purple apron, his striped bowtie. They refused to tell him what they thought he had stolen. We didn't get that information until my father took LoPri to court, and the company had to submit the information. All we knew was that my father was out of a job. Or knew when he finally told us, because he came in late for dinner that night, head hung low, unable to eat his meal or even tell us what was wrong.

I didn't think my father was a thief, even though it might be pretty tempting to take stuff, working in a store like that. Sometimes, though, lying in bed, I wondered just for a moment. But wouldn't he have given my sister the Barbie camper van and me the Sidney Crosby hockey stick? Wouldn't my mother have been happily grinding coffee beans in the kitchen while my dad was on the porch learning to play the banjo?

I felt bad for even thinking about it. And I thought, if his own kid could doubt for a second, then what did everybody else in town believe?

And I knew the answer. They thought a big company like LoPri couldn't be wrong.

~ 2 ~

The Third Floor

My mother worked, too. In fact, she had a better-paying job than my father, as a dental hygienist. That's the person (usually a woman) who cleans your teeth — scraping off the plaque, swabbing on the fluoride — and then when the dentist puts in a filling, handing over the instruments and suctioning up your spit.

Raising a family, as my parents often said, is expensive. My older brother was away at college, my older sister went to high school and took piano lessons and liked to go to movies every weekend, and my little sister refused to wear hand-medowns. They needed every penny of both salaries to "keep our ship afloat."

Our house wasn't as expensive as a house in a big city, but it was big, with fancy old brickwork and a veranda that went right around it and "three generous floors," as my dad always said.

My mom and dad both used to walk by this house on the way to school when they were kids. It was boarded up then and people said it was haunted, but both of them dreamed of living in it some day — something they discovered after they started dating in high school.

So when my mom was pregnant with me they finally bought it even though it meant a mortgage they could just manage and no vacations to Tahiti or Kathmandu for the next twenty years. But I loved our house which, after all, was the only house I had ever known.

Anyway, when my dad lost his job, we began to fall behind on our bills pretty quickly. Mom maxed out her credit card, the organic fruit and vegetable van wouldn't make its weekly stop at our house unless we paid in cash, and two months in a row we were late making the mortgage payments to the bank and were given a warning.

My parents never talked about these things in front of us kids, but I picked it all up anyway, including a word that I had never heard before and got to check off in my dictionary. Foreclosure. *(Foreclose: to bar or shut out upon non-payment of money due.)*

One day my older brother phoned home to ask if he could have money to buy a leather university jacket, and my dad went ballistic into the telephone. But afterwards he apologized and the next day he found his golf clubs in the garage and drove somewhere and came back without them and then casually mentioned at dinner that he had sent my brother the money for the jacket.

"A boy needs to feel like he belongs at college," Dad said.

By then my dad had started his case against LoPri. He was sure he would win. Or at least he said he was sure. But even if he did win, he didn't know if he would get his job back. He spent a lot of time in his workshop in the garage, building a rocking chair, fixing the lawnmower. (He had a lot of tools arranged above his workbench. Before he was hardware section manager of the LoPri store he had worked on the hardware floor, and he had been a little sorry to get promoted as he liked helping people.) When Dad did find work, it was a part-time sales position at a shoe store in the mall, and it only paid half as much as his manager position.

That was why my parents decided to rent out the third floor.

It was a good-sized floor, even if the walls began to slant halfway up because of the roof. Basically it was two long rooms with an archway between them. One of the rooms had a small sink, but there was no bathroom or kitchen. The stairs from the hall below came up through the floor. Four dormer windows gave it plenty of light.

Mom did the household accounts up there and also had her paints and easel and sewing machine, while my older sister often hung out up there with her friends. My little sister had her dollhouse there and our old puppet stage. My brother had left behind his drum kit when he went off to college. I used a folding bridge table to build plastic model airplanes, but I'd been losing interest lately and there was an unfinished Messerschmitt resting on it.

"So you see," Mom said at dinner one night, "we hardly use the third floor at all. We could rent it out to some nice single person, perhaps a young woman with her first job."

"I wouldn't take less than three hundred a month for it," Dad said. "We could cover our mortgage payments."

"But having a stranger in our house would be so creepy," said my older sister. "She'd use our bathroom. And our kitchen. Yuck."

"Yeah," said my little sister, who imitated everything my older sister did. "Yuck."

"We could put in that old hot plate and buy a little used fridge," my dad said. "But, yes, she would have to use the bathroom."

"She'd leave her make-up on the counter. And it would be all steamy from her showers."

I didn't say what I was thinking, that the person would stink up the bathroom and that stranger stink would be even worse than family stink. Because my mom said, "I guess, Horace," — that was my father's name — "we've pampered our children too much. They don't know what hardship is. When I was growing up, I had to share a room with my two sisters. When I was twelve years old I had to get up at six o'clock every morning to deliver newspapers."

"We've spoiled them rotten," my father agreed. "In the harvest season we had five or six men staying with us. I had to serve them their meals and clean up after."

"Okay, okay," my sister said. "I don't care. Rent the whole house. We can live in the garage."

"No," Mom said mildly. "We'll just rent the third floor."

"Just don't expect me to become her best friend or something," my sister said.

"Me neither," said my little sister.

"No," Dad said. "We just expect you to be polite. That means you, too, Randolph."

Did I mention that my name is Randolph? That I have a name used only by characters in old black-and-white movies?

"I know," I said.

~ 3 ~

Not a Fish

THE FIRST THING my parents did was to put up signs at the grocery store, the community center and on the bulletin board in front of the local newspaper office.

Third-floor flat for rent. Two spacious rooms. Small kitchen, share bath. Suit non-smoking, fastidious, quiet person who likes children.

A week went by without a single phone call.

"Maybe you're being too fussy," I suggested to them at breakfast. "How about this? Suit chain-smoking, noisy slob who hates kids."

Only my dad laughed out loud. But at dinner time he couldn't hide his big grin.

"We got a call for the apartment today."

"We did?" Mom said. "Why didn't you say anything? Thank goodness. If we can get the first and last month's rent right away we'll make our bills this month. Who is she?"

"Yes, who is she?" asked my sister. "Does she work? God, I hope I don't know her from the jeans store or somewhere. That would be so embarrassing. Yuck."

"The name of our tenant is Mr. Karp."

"*Mr.?* It's a man? Double yuck. I guess it wouldn't be so bad if he's young. Is he young?"

"I'd say he's not much past the age of fifty."

"Fifty!"

"Isn't a carp a kind of fish?" I asked.

"That's when it's spelled with a C. This is K-A-R-P."

"But you said 'our tenant,' Horace," my mother said. "We haven't even met him yet."

"Oh, yes, we have. Or at least I have. I met him here on my lunch break. We had a very nice chat. Well, he's not all that talkative. But he's perfectly nice and with good manners. He has excellent references and works at Macintosh's."

"At that musty old department store where the clothes are ten years out of date?" my sister said. "What does he do?"

"He runs the complaints department. Actually, he *is* the complaints department. I suppose that explains his even temperament. You'd need it, dealing with angry and upset people all day long. I admit, he's a little eccentric."

"You mean he's weird?" I asked.

"No, I mean eccentric. He dresses in an old-fashioned way and he has a funny little moustache — he's a small man generally — and he speaks in a rather formal manner. He has an arrangement at Macintosh's and takes most of his meals in their restaurant.

So he'll only be cooking a little on weekends. If you want to know the truth, I was worried that he wouldn't find the house up to his standard. He noticed the dust on the bookshelf in the hallway — he ran his finger along it. I believe it was your turn to dust this week, Randolph. He looked at the drums and the easel on the third floor and asked if our children were beatniks."

"Beatniks!" Mom said. "I haven't heard that word for decades."

"And look," Dad said.

He took a folded slip of paper from his pocket. When he unfolded it we all saw that it was a check for six hundred dollars.

"First and last month's rent," he said and smiled.

"Oh, Horace, that's wonderful. That's just what we need."

"Until I win my court case," my father reminded her.

"Yes, I mean until then, of course."

"This will interest you, Randolph," my father said to me. "Mr. Karp is some sort of collector."

"A collector of what?" Mom asked. "Books? Pottery?"

"I can't remember. Or perhaps he didn't tell me. He asked if he could bring in some shelves for his collection. Whatever it is, he's got quite a lot of them. Almost three hundred."

"Almost three hundred!" I blurted out. "Wow."

Naturally I looked forward to seeing what Mr. Karp would bring when he moved in on Monday, which was the first of the month. I spent a good part of the weekend speculating hopefully on the kind of thing he might collect. Insect specimens? Strange musical instruments that you blew with your nose or plucked with your feet? Shrunken heads? I just hoped it wasn't something boring like stamps. Or souvenir spoons. Please, don't let it be souvenir spoons!

On Monday something really lucky happened. I woke up sick. Not so sick that I felt like throwing up. Just sick enough with a low fever and a sore throat to stay home from school. Dad had to go to the shoe store and Mom to the dentist's office, but I convinced them both that I would be well enough to stay by myself. They could call me every hour and if I needed anything I could phone Mrs. Tenney, our neighbor.

My mother called Mrs. Tenney and my dad fixed me a tuna fish sandwich which he left in the fridge for lunch, and my older sister said what a big faker I was, and my little sister made me a card with a picture of a frog on it that said *"hop hop hop hop get well I want to take ballet goodbye."* Just before he left, Dad reminded me (as if I could have forgotten) that Mr. Karp was going to move in this morning and already had a key.

My bedroom faced the back of the house, so I took up a post at the bay window of my parents' room to keep watch on the street.

It was an hour before a small green moving van pulled into our gravel drive. The doors opened and out came two burly men in T-shirts and a much smaller man wearing a black suit and a small-brimmed hat. He did not help the moving men but stood by the open doors of the van and directed them with brisk movements and a voice too quiet for me to hear even when I cranked open the window.

Out came a dresser, a bureau, a small desk, a single bed and mattress, an old portable record player (the kind that played vinyl records), a file cabinet, a chair and three-legged table, and shelves. He pointed to whatever remained in the van and I could hear him say, "No, leave those until the room is in order, if you please." Then he followed the movers into the house.

I stayed in my parents' room as they passed up and down the stairs. I could hear the moving of furniture up above me, and then three sets of footsteps going down again.

Only now did Mr. Karp oversee the unloading of a series of wooden crates, each marked FRAGILE and also PERISHABLE, a word I didn't know.

"Careful now! Don't tip the crate, if you please," said Mr. Karp as they navigated up the veranda steps.

PERISHABLE
FRAGILE

It took the men six trips to bring up all the crates. Then I watched Mr. Karp sign a paper on a clipboard. The van drove off and Mr. Karp came inside, locking the front door of the house behind him. He came up the stairs, past the second floor and up to the third where I heard the trap door close.

I did not see Mr. Karp again that day. Instead, I heard sounds coming from the third floor. Beethoven's Ninth Symphony (the only symphony I knew) from the record player. A crowbar pulling open the wooden crates.

No, that isn't true. I saw him one time, when he brought down all the dismantled crates tied in bundles and put them in the back of the garage. I knew that my father had given him permission to use some space as storage.

Mr. Karp was just coming out of the garage for the last time when my father arrived home carrying a bag of groceries. He put down the groceries and stretched out his hand to shake Mr. Karp's.

Mr. Karp hesitated a moment, as if my

father's hand might be sticky or cold, but then he reached out his own and gave my father a quick shake.

"Settled in, have you, Mr. Karp?"

"Just about," Mr. Karp answered.

"Nothing broken in the move, I hope," Dad asked.

"No, thank goodness. Always a fear, you know. Always a very great fear for someone with my particular interest. Well, I've still got a lot to do."

"I'm sure. Well, welcome aboard, Mr. Karp."

The two of them came into the house together — my father heading to the kitchen and Mr. Karp to his apartment, which was how I already thought of the third floor.

As soon as his door was closed I hurried into my own room and slipped into bed, in preparation for my father coming up to see how I was feeling.

~ 4 ~

Perishable

My father and mother were happy with Mr. Karp as a tenant, and even my sister didn't complain. He did not slam doors, did not walk through the house in muddy shoes (Mr. Karp wore rubber overshoes when it rained and always removed them at the door), did not leave hairs in the bathroom sink.

The only signs of him at all were the faint sounds of his symphonies, the occasional creaking of a floorboard and the disappearance of the mail left for him on the little table by the front door.

Mr. Karp did not get any personal mail

— invitations, postcards, envelopes with a handwritten address. He received copies of a newsletter called *The Drip* (I couldn't see what it was about, as it was folded up and stapled) and small brown envelopes from someone named R.B. Purcell, Reliable Agent. Twice in the first month he also received small packages by special delivery. Like the crates, they were marked FRAGILE and PERISHABLE, and when Mr. Karp found one of these on the little table, signed for by my father or my sister, he would hurry up to his apartment, clutching it in his hands.

(Perishable: naturally subject to speedy decay. That which is transitory. Things liable to decay; said chiefly of foodstuffs in transit.)

What in the heck was Mr. Karp collecting? Bagels? Exotic fruit? Chocolate cream puffs?

Although he was neat and quiet, Mr. Karp was not invisible. In the cool evenings he liked to sit in one of the rocking chairs on our veranda just as the sun was going down. He would drink a small glass of sherry while he read his latest copy of *The Drip*. He had asked permission to use the veranda and always took up a place along the west side of the house, in order to see the sunset and also to be less noticeable to us in the house.

I wanted to go up to Mr. Karp and speak to him, but something always held me back. He didn't look grumpy or mean, but he didn't look particularly friendly, either. I couldn't get up the nerve to do it.

Instead, I went up to my own room to look over my collections. My beer-bottle caps, now at fifty-nine, included a Moretti from Italy and a Löwenbräu from Germany, with a tiny picture of a woman in a white dress standing beside a lion (whatever that had to do with beer).

In my dictionary, I looked up a new word — (*Lassitude: weariness of body or mind, lack of energy, languor*) — and put a tick next to it.

The truth is, none of my collections seemed very interesting to me any more.

Was there something else I could collect? Cereal boxes were boring. My parents wouldn't let me keep cigarette lighters. Old cameras might be interesting but would cost money.

Roofing shingles? Dead butterflies? Umbrellas?

Dumb ideas, every one.

~ 5 ~
The Complaints Department

On Saturday afternoons I liked to throw a baseball around with my dad. On this Saturday, about six weeks after Mr. Karp came to live in our house, I got my glove from the front closet and found Dad in the kitchen, a stack of dull-looking books in front of him.

"Want to help me practice hitting some grounders?" I said.

"Maybe later, Randolph. I've got a lot of reading to do on my case. You'd be surprised how complicated the law is. Why don't you head over to the field beside Fletcher's Variety? There's always a pick-up game on Saturdays, isn't there?"

"Sure," I said. "I'll see you later."

"Hit one over the fence," Dad said. He always told me to hit one over the fence when I went to the field to play, even though there was no fence.

"Dad," I said, "do you think it's worth it? I mean, all the trouble."

But my dad didn't answer. He was already too engrossed in the open book on the table to hear me.

Outside, I hooked my glove on the handle of my bicycle. But I didn't head over to the field. I turned right instead and pedaled furiously to Queen Street and turned right again.

Two blocks later I stopped in front of Macintosh's Department Store.

Macintosh's was the oldest business in our town. *Est. 1911*, as it said beside the door. In most towns like ours, my father had told me, places like Macintosh's had closed down long ago. Most people preferred to shop at the big discount stores off the highway, places like LoPri, which my father was taking to court, only the case was moving forward with the speed of a "very excited snail." Dad said that Macintosh's survival was some kind of miracle and that he wouldn't be surprised if it went bankrupt one of these days.

Everything about it did seem old-fashioned, from the mannequins in the windows with their plastic 1950s hairdos to the creaking elevator that had an actual elevator operator who would ask you what floor you wanted.

I parked my bike and went through the revolving door. Inside, a saleswoman with a perfume bottle was spraying people as they came in. But she took one look at me and didn't spray. On one of the marble pillars was a directory of departments, and I stood reading it.

First floor: Watches, Jewelry, Handbags, Hats, Men's Suits, Rainwear, Perfume. Second floor: Women's Clothing, Shoes, Kids' Clothing, Toys, Small Appliances, Packaged Foods, Restaurant. Third floor: Furniture, Large Appliances, Bedding, Final Sale Items, Complaints Department.

My first stop was packaged foods. I asked the elevator operator for the second floor and he pushed the lever. He wore a nice red uniform with shiny brass buttons. I wondered where an elevator operator could get a uniform these days and whether he had to pay for it himself.

On the second floor I walked past mannequins of women wearing only bras and underpants and felt my face turn red.

Finally I reached the packaged foods department. There were small cans of fish, tins of cookies and small boxes of English tea. I picked up a package of dry-looking biscuits. What were biscuits, anyway? They weren't really crackers and they weren't really cookies. But I picked up the box and took it to the lady behind the cash register. She told me they cost three dollars and seventy-two cents.

I counted out the money in quarters, nickels, dimes and two pennies. My pants pocket was a lot lighter after that. The lady asked if I would like her to wrap the biscuits as a gift. Who would give biscuits as a gift? But I just said, "No, thank you," and she put the biscuits into an enormous Macintosh's bag. I could have fit three basketballs in that bag.

Carrying the bag, I went back to the elevator. The doors opened and I got in and asked the elevator operator for the third floor.

"Yes, sir," he said and pushed the lever.

I got out on the third floor, went past rows of washing machines and stoves, past shelves of blenders, past banged-up boxes with Sale stickers on them, and reached a little sign hanging from the ceiling.

COMPLAINTS DEPARTMENT

The sign pointed down a narrow corridor.

With the Macintosh bag knocking against my legs, I walked down the corridor. For some reason I felt as if I was walking to my own firing squad. I tried to put my feet down gently but my steps echoed.

At the end of the corridor was a window

with a counter behind it, and as I got closer I saw that the counter was bare except for one of those small bells that you had to tap to make ring.

I lightly tapped the bell. It made a tiny ping, and I was thinking that I would have to hit it harder when Mr. Karp's head suddenly appeared from one side.

"Good afternoon. May I be of service?"

Mr. Karp didn't seem to recognize me. I took a step back. Speak clearly and forcefully, I told myself.

"I want to return these biscuits."

"There is no need to shout, young man. I hear you very well."

His mouth turned down, as if he had tasted something disagreeable. He had a sort of interesting face: thick eyebrows that moved independently of one another, a moustache that twitched, eyes that narrowed or grew round. I had seen his expression change when I watched him read his latest copy of *The Drip* on the veranda.

Now he motioned with his hand for me to put the bag up on the counter. I did so.

Mr. Karp peered into the bag and then daintily removed the box. It was a long rectangle, with pictures of biscuits all over it and the name *Darson's 100% Digestible Invigoration Biscuits,* tightly wrapped in cellophane.

Mr. Karp held the box close to his face, as if he were going to sniff it. Then he put it down on the counter.

"I see," he said, reaching behind him. Without looking, he took a clipboard from a nail on the wall. "If I might ask a few questions."

"Sure," I said.

"Date of purchase?"

"Today. Ten minutes ago."

He looked at me and then back at the clipboard.

"Reason for purchase?"

"To eat them."

"Did you open the box?"

This seemed to me a pretty dumb question since the cellophane was still on it. I said, "No, I did not."

"Did you damage the item in any way?

BIS
100%
BIS
ABC
THE

For example, did you drop it? Did your pet get hold of it? Did you ride over it on your bicycle? Did you drop it in a bathtub full of water?"

"I never even took it out of the store."

Again he looked at me, but this time he kept looking at me and did not refer to the clipboard.

"One last question. What is the reason for your returning it?"

I felt his eyes hard on mine, unblinking. I myself blinked and looked down at my shoes.

"Because I discovered something about it."

"Discovered something? What did you discover?"

"I discovered ... I discovered that it's ... perishable."

"You say that you discovered that it is perishable?"

I looked up again. "That's right. That's exactly why I'm returning these biscuits."

Now it was my turn to stare at Mr. Karp. Did he flinch? Did he show any recognition of this word that I knew only because it was stenciled on his crates and his little packages?

Something flashed across his face, but it was impossible to read. With pen in hand, he began to write on the clipboard, speaking aloud the words.

"Customer … discovered … item … to be … perishable."

Mr. Karp turned the clipboard toward me and held out the pen.

"If you would just sign at the bottom."

I wrote my name. My signature looked very babyish, like I had just learned how to write cursive. Mr. Karp took the clipboard and the pen back, signed the page himself, tore out the carbon copy underneath and handed it to me.

"For your records," he said. He hung up the clipboard again and removed the box of biscuits and the bag from the counter.

"How would you like it, then?"

"Pardon me?"

"Your money. How would you like it?"

"Oh. In quarters, dimes, nickels and pennies, please."

A money drawer popped open from under the counter. Mr. Karp counted out the change and dropped it into my cupped hand. I put the change back in my pocket where it weighed heavily once more.

"Thank you," Mr. Karp said, "for shopping at Macintosh's."

"You're welcome."

I began to turn away.

"Young man?"

"Yes?" I turned around again.

"Many valuable things in the world — perhaps the most valuable things — are perishable."

And then he walked away from the window.

~ 6 ~
The Collection

Mr. Karp and I never spoke about our meeting at the complaints department of Macintosh's Department Store, but it made a difference between us. After that, whenever we passed — for example when I was leaving the bathroom and he was waiting to go in, or when he was rocking on the veranda reading the latest issue of *The Drip* and I skateboarded by — we would nod sagely to each other. *(Sagely: wisely, discreetly.)*

And then, finally, we spoke.

It was a Sunday afternoon. My sisters were out with friends, my mom was playing tennis at the public courts, my dad was taking a nap. I took my cigar boxes of beer-bottle caps out to the west side of the veranda and sat cross-legged on the boards. I proceeded to lay out the bottle caps, not according to color or some other silly system, but according to place of origin.

I had a large world map which I spread out, and I placed the caps as close to the cities they came from as I could. I worked slowly and deliberately, using our *Britnell's World Atlas and Gazetteer* to look up places I wasn't sure about or couldn't see on the small scale of the spread-out map.

I was a little more than halfway done when Mr. Karp came out of the house, careful not to let the screen door slam behind him. I did not look up but knew he was moving toward his usual rocker. His footsteps stopped, turned, then came toward me. I could see his black shoes and the cuffs of his trousers as he stood on the other side of the map.

Only then did I notice that his shoes,

although very polished, were quite worn and needed to be reheeled, and that the cuffs of his trousers had been neatly mended with nearly invisible thread.

When I looked up I saw that he was looking down at the beer caps on the map.

"What have we here, Randolph?"

I'd never heard him say my name before. I didn't even know that he knew it, although of course he must have heard my family calling me ten times a day.

"It's my collection," I said. "Or one of them, anyway."

"I see you have some good caps there. Dutch, Chinese. You've kept them in good condition, too. Of course when I was a boy they were harder to obtain. You couldn't buy foreign beers in the store."

"You collected beer-bottle caps?"

"Yes, I did."

"How many did you have?"

"At the peak? Four hundred and seventy-two."

"Wow!"

"But I was nineteen by then, much older

than you. Tell me, what are your other collections?"

"Writing instruments. And words — in the dictionary, I mean."

"A kind of conceptual collection, then."

"I used to collect snowglobes when I was younger. But I got bored with them."

"The common boyhood run. I understand your waning enthusiasm."

"I haven't had any new good beer-bottle caps for a while. It's kind of bugging me."

"Naturally you feel some frustration. That, I'm afraid, is a frequent emotion felt by the collector. We aren't long satisfied by what we have. A new acquisition thrills us but for a short time and then soon we hunger for another. It is a feeling that gnaws at us like a parasite in the stomach."

"Yuck."

"Yuck indeed. But tracking down the new addition, hovering over it, deliriously hoping. And then finally having it in your grasp — what a delicious thrill. I believe that you understand what I mean, Randolph."

I wasn't sure that I did understand, but I tried to look as if I did.

"I'd like to start a new collection but I don't know what," I said.

"Don't rush into it, Randolph. Choose wisely. Once you choose it becomes an obligation, a burden as much as a pleasure. I myself did not settle on my current subject until some twelve years ago. But I made a good choice. It has kept me hopping!"

I waited. He said nothing more.

I looked across the lawn to the next house and said, "What do you collect, Mr. Karp?"

He began to make an odd, half-swallowed sort of noise, and for a second I thought that he was choking.

But he wasn't choking. He was laughing.

"I haven't told you, have I? Well, it isn't something that I like to just bandy about to anyone. Most people don't appreciate this little passion of mine. But someone like you, Randolph, that's different. I know you will understand. Would you like to see my collection?"

"Yes!" I began to put the beer-bottle caps

back into the cigar boxes as quickly as I could.

"Slow down, young man. You don't want to scratch the designs on those caps. Proper care is as important as acquiring your examples in the first place. I'll help you and then you may go and ask your father for permission to visit with me. It's always important to get parental agreement, you know."

"Okay," I said. At last all the caps were back in the boxes and I raced into the house, slamming the screen door behind me. I hurled myself upstairs and was about to drop the cigar boxes on my bed when I thought better of it and placed them down gently instead.

Then I ran down the hall and burst into my parents' bedroom.

Where my dad was snoring on his back, wearing his boxer shorts and socks.

"Hey, Dad?"

"Ah … ahhh."

"Are you awake?"

"Hmm."

"Can I have a visit with Mr. Karp? He invited me."

"Who?"

"Mr. Karp."

"O … okay … ahhh."

Dad rolled over and began snoring again. I couldn't understand why adults liked to sleep in the afternoon, as if they were babies needing naps.

I raced back down the hall and almost collided with Mr. Karp, who was coming up the stairs.

"Careful, Randolph! Steadiness. Patience. These habits reward the collector."

"Yes, sir. My dad says I can come up."

"Very good. This way then. I don't have to tell you to be careful, not to wave your arms around and such. As you know, my collection is fragile. *And* perishable."

He winked at me and then began to climb the stairs to the third floor while I followed behind.

I felt breathless with excitement. Mr. Karp pushed open the trap door and disappeared into the square of light. I went after, emerging in the sink room of his little apartment. I saw the little refrigerator, the sink. A bed with a night table and lamp and a neat pile of *The Drip.* The record player and a few other things.

But it was the other room that I wanted to see, and when I looked at Mr. Karp, he nodded and motioned for me to go through the archway.

And as soon as I went through, I was dumbstruck. *(Dumbstruck: made silent, mute, losing the ability to speak.)* Mr. Karp had laid a worn but handsome Persian carpet on the floor. In the middle was a chair and the small antique table with three legs.

And every wall of the room was lined with shelves.

The shelves were narrower than bookshelves. On them, row upon row upon row, were glass containers. They were about the size of small goldfish bowls only they were square. And each of them was filled with water.

Clear water in most of them, but not all. In some the water was tinged with yellow

(some pale, others deeper) or violet or green or blue. The afternoon light, slanting in through the two big dormer windows, shone through them, casting colored light everywhere.

I felt as if I were underwater, or in a submarine with hundreds of tiny windows looking out to the mysterious depths of the ocean.

"Go on," said Mr. Karp. "Take a closer look."

I stepped gingerly up to one of the shelves. Only as I got closer did I see that each container had a glass stopper. Also that a small label was affixed near the base of each one.

I read the label in front of me.

Ditch water from St. Louis, Missouri,
after the tornado of 1896

The water in the container was greenish and murky, and strangely beautiful.

I read the label next to it.

Gulf of Oman, near Cha Bahar,
Iran, 1993

And the one next to it.

Round Pond,
Kensington Gardens, London,
during miniature boat races, 1873

After that I began to move around the room, reading labels here and there, stopping to look more closely at the samples in various containers. Putting my face right up to them, I could see that one looked almost milky, another tinted the faintest raspberry. A few had bits of debris in them — wood fibers turned feathery or a few grains of sand on the bottom. One had a single piece of blue beach glass, the edges worn smooth. But most were just water.

Delaware River,
one hour after George Washington's
crossing, 1776

Swimming pool,
1980 Olympic Games, Moscow

Melted from Montreal Ice Storm of 1998

Bathwater of Sarah Bernhardt
after performance of Cleopatra, 1891

I said, "Who was Sarah Bernhardt?"

"The most famous stage actress of the nineteenth century. They called her the Divine Sarah, and she was more famous in Paris, London and New York than pop stars are today. To understand her tragic roles better she used to sleep in a coffin."

"That's creepy."

"Later in life, she had a terrible injury and the doctors had to amputate her leg. It is said that a famous showman offered her ten thousand dollars to display her leg to the public."

"Gross!"

"She refused. Instead, she continued to perform and became even more famous than before."

I took another look at Sarah Bernhardt's bathwater and then backed away from the shelf so that I could take in the entire room.

I felt weird emotions running through me — excitement, awe, stupefaction. (*Stupefaction: a sense of overwhelming astonishment.*) Mr. Karp stood just behind the table and I could tell by his expression that he was seeing his collection through my eyes. I guess he didn't often have a chance to show it to someone who wouldn't think he was a total oddball.

Well, just because I appreciated it didn't mean I didn't think that he was an oddball.

"A collection of water," I said. "I never would have guessed, not in a million years. It's got to be the only one in the world."

Mr. Karp took his handkerchief from his pocket and touched his forehead.

"On the contrary, Randolph. On the contrary."

~ 7 ~

THE REVILED RAVELSON

I WANTED TO KNOW what Mr. Karp meant but at that moment I heard my mother calling me from downstairs. The rest of the family had returned home and my parents wanted to take us on one of our Sunday drives. I hated being wedged in the back seat with my sisters while my parents said things like, "Isn't that a gorgeous farmhouse?" and "Kids, look at that field of canola!" Then it was home again for an enforced bath and hairwashing, and a "proper" bedtime before Monday-morning school.

So it was three days before I found Mr. Karp on the veranda with his newsletter.

That's when he told me more about water collecting.

Although it wasn't well known, Mr. Karp explained, water collecting was pursued by people in Europe, in North and South America, in Africa and Asia. They had conventions, dealers who sold containers, books of history. The central association in Zurich, Switzerland, oversaw the authenticity of samples (each one had to have a signed and sealed certificate).

Mr. Karp told me that he himself was considered the second-foremost collector in the northeast. He showed me his own name in several back issues of *The Drip*, the association newsletter.

If Mr. Karp was the second-foremost collector in the northeast, I asked, then who was the first?

"Ravelson," Mr. Karp said, his lips pressed tight.

Mr. Karp did not go to places himself to get his samples. Only collectors who couldn't afford the high cost of fine examples would actually scoop water from, say, Lake

Michigan or a rain puddle during the Rose Bowl parade, although Mr. Karp told me that this was an honorable way to begin. He relied on various agents — in particular one named R.B. Purcell — to find what he was looking for. Really rare samples were pursued by more than one collector.

Just recently, Ravelson had "stolen" a sample of water from the River Seine taken on the very day that Paris was liberated from the Nazis.

Most of the time Mr. Karp did not just say "Ravelson" but "the Reviled Ravelson," as if that were his actual name. The rivalry between the two men was mentioned frequently in the North America column of *The Drip* and there was even a photograph of Ravelson smiling and holding up the River Seine sample.

After that, I made it a habit to meet Mr. Karp on the veranda after dinner, although the evenings were getting cooler. He would be wrapped in a frayed sweater, and if a new sample had arrived that day, he would show it to me.

The most impressive was water from a drinking bottle used by Jackie Robinson, the first black major-league baseball player, during the last game of the 1955 World Series. Mr. Karp didn't have to tell me about Jackie Robinson. I already knew about how the fans and other players called him names because he was black, and that he was the best base stealer of all time.

"Jeez," I said, holding the container up to the light. "That's better than any old baseball card."

"A very nice sample. It took months of negotiations to acquire it. And it wasn't cheap, either. I was finally going to buy a new suit and a winter coat. But I'd rather have this. Still, it doesn't take the sting away from losing the Seine sample that the Reviled Ravelson stole from me."

As he spoke, his voice took on a bitter and sneering tone that was not at all like Mr. Karp. It was as if the very thought of Ravelson turned him into another kind of person.

One evening, when it began to snow and

Mr. Karp wore a hat and gloves on the veranda, he told me that certificates of authenticity only became mandatory in 1962. That was when an agent named Alfred Linkster was discovered to have sold fake samples, including one that was supposed to be water from the pot used to boil a leg of mutton for William Shakespeare while he was writing *Romeo and Juliet*. Hundreds of samples were declared false and dozens of collectors were ruined. Other collectors quit, and many began to sell off their collections for bargain prices.

"That," Mr. Karp said, brushing a snowflake from his moustache, "was how I built my own collection. They lost heart but I was young and had courage. And that is why I have the second-foremost collection in the northeast."

"After Ravelson," I said.

A long pause from Mr. Karp.

"Yes," he finally said.

~ 8 ~

Mr. Karp Takes a Trip

It may sound as if I spent a lot of time with Mr. Karp. But I was mostly doing other things. The hockey season started, and because we didn't have much money — what with my dad working only part-time as a shoe salesman and also having to pay the lawyer in his court case — I had to go to three different swap meets to find equipment that fit me. Usually Dad went to the games with me, but this year he was too busy reading up on wrongful dismissal, so I had to get a lift with one of my teammates.

And then there was school. I had to draw

the circulatory system of the frog. I had to act in a play in French. I had to write a short story and a book report.

I even had homework in art.

I could never understand why teachers hated white space. Whenever I painted a picture for art class, the teacher never allowed me to leave the sky white or the walls of the house blank. She always made me fill it in and when I did my brush would always mess up the people or trees and spoil the whole thing. Happened every time.

And it happened this time, too.

I was sprawled on the floor of my room, finishing a watercolor painting of my bike which was due the next day. I thought it looked just fine with the background white but I was carefully painting in a green hill behind it, careful to stop my brush just as I got to the edge of the bike.

I was trying to fill in the triangular spaces between the spokes when a knock on the door made my hand jump and I washed a streak of green right over the wheel.

The door opened a little.

"Randolph?"

"Hi, Mr. Karp," I said, sitting up.

He stepped into the room.

"I have some exciting news and I just have to share it with you. Would you care to come upstairs a moment? Unless you're too busy, of course."

"No, no, I'm coming," I said, happy to take a break.

We went up the stairs into Mr. Karp's apartment and straight into the room that held his collection. It was after dark and there was only a small lamp with a green shade glowing on the file cabinet. I felt like I was underwater at midnight.

"I've found it," he said.

"Found what?"

"It's within my grasp."

"What's within your grasp?"

"The sample that I've spent eight years searching for. A unique sample. There is only one."

"But what is it, Mr. Karp?"

"Melted snow."

"Snow?"

"Yes, snow. Taken from the upturned hat of Napoleon Bonaparte during the Russian campaign."

"The French general, right?"

"He decided to invade Russia, you see, but when he arrived in Moscow he discovered that the city had been abandoned and all the food and supplies taken or burned. He had no choice but to retreat. The French troops froze in the cold Russian winter. The Russian soldiers attacked them. They ran out of food and had to eat their horses."

"As if the horses wanted to go in the first place!" I said.

"It was the last day of October, 1812. Napoleon's troops had just lost a skirmish and he was so angry that he kicked his famous tri-cornered hat out of the tent. Snow was falling. After a while an army captain came by and scooped the snow out of the hat. When the snow melted he poured it into his flask. He wrote a letter about it that very night to his wife in Paris, thus creating a document. The next day the captain received a saber wound just under his heart and died, but his sword, medals, letters, and the flask were sent back to his wife. For generations the flask was passed down until it ended up in the hands of a Dutch art dealer who traded it for an Italian painting. It has changed hands no less than twelve times since. For the past three years it has been owned by the president of a Japanese bank, who kept it in a vault. Now it is in the hands of his widow. It is a magnificent sample. Nothing in my collection compares to it."

"And the reviled Ravelson?" I asked.

"Nothing in his collection, either. That one sample will make me the foremost collector in the northeast."

"Wow. Go for it, Mr. Karp."

"It is not so easy. The widow is eighty-three years old and very difficult. I've been courting her for months and at last she thinks she wants to sell. I have agreed to name it the Nakajima Sample in honor of her late husband. Now she only has to sign the sales contract. I received a telegram from Purcell this morning. He urges me to come myself. Meeting her in person will tip the balance."

"You're going to Japan?"

"Kyoto. I have taken a week's leave of absence from Macintosh's. My plane departs tomorrow morning at nine. It is a twelve-hour journey. I will come back next Saturday, Randolph. And if I am successful I will be able to show you the Nakajima Sample before anyone else. Snow from Napoleon's hat! Just think of it."

I did think of it. Not only then, but for half the night. I even dreamed about it.

In my dream, I am a boy in Napoleon's army, running errands for Napoleon himself. I stand outside his tent, shivering with cold, listening to his angry voice. Something flies out of the tent and hits me on the cheek. It is Napoleon's hat. It has landed upside down and now snow drifts down into it. Wishing to return it, I reach out but my feet slip and I fall face downwards, the snow pushing into my nose and mouth. I shake off the snow and stretch a hand forward but a gust of wind carries the hat forward, just out of reach ...

When I woke up in the morning, Mr. Karp had already left for the airport.

~ 9 ~

Weird Thoughts

THIS IS WHAT I THOUGHT about while Mr. Karp was on his way to Japan.

Water was not actually perishable.

At least, I didn't think it was. It didn't go bad the way a hamburger or a chocolate eclair would. It just changed form. It evaporated and became a gas. It froze and became a solid. It moved down rivers and waterfalls. It floated off in clouds. But it didn't really go away.

Maybe Mr. Karp knew this. Maybe it was just easier to mark his crates *Perishable* than *May Evaporate*.

Here's something else I thought about. To me, Japan was really far away. Half way around the world. But to a kid living in Kyoto, Japan, it wasn't him who was far away. It was *me*.

Here's something else I thought.

Mr. Karp was crazy.

Maybe all collectors were a little bit crazy. It didn't matter what they collected: coffee mugs with funny sayings on them, license plates, cuckoo clocks, stuffed owls, books on mind reading. You surrounded yourself with all this stuff. You made a kind of world of it. But you were never really happy because you couldn't own everything. Your world could never be complete. Somebody else's world was always going to be better than yours.

Then one day you would die.

And what would happen to your collection then? Maybe the individual things would be sold or given away. Maybe, if they weren't valuable to anyone else (like a collection of long underwear or used batteries), they would just be chucked out.

But until then, you worried. Worried that somebody else had a better collection, or that last Saturday when you couldn't go to the flea market you missed something, or that your collection might be stolen, or burned up in a fire, or might even evaporate. That it might perish before you did.

I really did have a lot of weird thoughts while Mr. Karp was on his way to Japan.

~10~

Our Day in Court

Mr. Karp did not come back on the Saturday. Two days later my dad said that something must have held him up.

"He's probably enjoying the sights. Maybe he's become a fan of kabuki, the traditional form of Japanese theater. All I can say is it's a good thing he's paid up on his rent."

A person can't remain excited about something forever, and as the days went by I started to think less about Mr. Karp and the Nakajima Sample. Our hockey team began to win a few games. Dad finally came to see me play and I scored a goal in the last minute of a tied game. Collecting things started to seem pretty ridiculous to me. Why had I ever been interested?

As another week went by, though, my parents began to wonder what had happened to Mr. Karp, and whether he was really going to be back in time to pay the next month's rent. Mail began to pile up on the little front table: a few bills, copies of *The Drip*.

Even so, our attention wasn't really on Mr. Karp, because my father's court case was finally about to come to an end. All the evidence had been submitted, the witnesses had testified, and now it was up to the judge to make his decision.

A few days later, I was sitting in my classroom after lunch when I looked up and saw my dad at the door, whispering to my teacher. Dad called me over and in the hallway he told me that he had received a phone call from the courthouse. The judge was going to give his decision. My mother and sisters were already in the car. Even my older brother had come by train all the way from college.

From the passenger seat, my mother reached back to run her hand through my hair. She wet her finger and rubbed a dirt smudge off my face. Nobody spoke.

We walked up to the courthouse. My parents each held one of my little sister's hands, and my older sister shocked me by taking my hand. We were early and took seats at the front.

The courtroom looked like I expected it to from TV except that it was more drab. The half-closed blinds on the high windows were dusty. The judge's desk was large but plain. The chairs we sat in were the sort of stacking chairs we used in the school auditorium.

Slowly other people drifted in: the court clerk, the stenographer who used a little typing machine to record what people said, a guard. Then the LoPri people — three lawyers, the store manager, and a vice-president of the company who had flown in from Austin, Texas.

My dad's own lawyer only rushed in at the last minute, stuffing papers into his briefcase.

The last person to come in was the judge, and we all had to stand up. He was a big man with a pointy nose, and he looked at us sourly and then shuffled the files on his desk.

The clerk called the court into session. The judge asked if both parties were present, and then he made a speech. At least it sounded like a speech to me.

He said the evidence showed clearly that the LoPri Company had serious problems with its inventory control. This problem was the fault of the store manager and the head office. Certain items — a metal gardening shed, a DVD collection of *I Love Lucy* television shows, a Barbie camper van, five bags of red licorice, a pink imitation Christmas tree with musical angel, a coffee-bean grinder, a Sidney Crosby hockey stick, a pair of steel-toed workboots and a five-string banjo with instruction manual — had gone missing. Whether they had been sold or had never actually existed the judge could not say, but there was no proof that my father or anyone else had stolen

them. In fact, all the witnesses had spoken of my father as a dedicated, honest and hard-working employee.

As a result, the judge said, he was ruling in favor of my father. The LoPri Company had to pay him his wages for all the months since he was fired. They had to pay his legal fees. They had to pay an additional sum of twenty-five thousand dollars as compensation for damage to his reputation and the suffering caused to him and his family. And they had to give him his job back.

When my dad heard the verdict he couldn't stop himself from yelling, "Yippee!" right in the courtroom. My mother and my older sister cried. My little sister and my brother and I jumped up and down.

That night we went to my dad's favorite Chinese restaurant to celebrate. In all those months we hadn't been to a restaurant once.

While we were eating, my brother said, "Are you really going to go back and work for those bums?"

"As a matter of fact, I'm not," Dad said.

"I'm going to open my own hardware store in town. Right where the old one used to be. I can do it now with the money the company has to pay us. I've even found a group of independent hardware stores who do their buying together to lower costs. Your dad is going to be his own boss."

I was so excited that night that I could hardly stay still in bed. Dad came in to say goodnight and, sitting on the end of my bed, he apologized for spending so little time with me. He said that we would go to a movie together and that he was going to start coming to all my hockey games again.

I just lay there feeling happy, which is why, very late, I heard the front door open and somebody come up the stairs and keep going.

Mr. Karp had come back.

~11~

A Quite Significant Decision

Usually I woke up when the sun slanted through my blinds, but the next morning I slept in. I'd had a night of roiling dreams. (*Roiling: stirred up, disturbed.*) All I could remember was that I was swimming deep underwater trying to catch up with Mr. Karp, who was swimming to Japan. But Mr. Karp was always ahead of me, his trousered legs kicking like a frog.

My mother had to wake me up and tell me I would be late for school. I threw on my clothes, grabbed a banana and rode my bike at top speed. Which meant that once more I did not get to see Mr. Karp.

During lunch I went into the library and found a book about Napoleon. Born in 1769 in Corsica, he had become a French army officer and fought during the French Revolution. He had a series of brilliant victories as a general. Then in 1799 he took over power in France and became a military dictator. He made reforms in government and education. And he fought more victorious military battles, at least until the disastrous invasion of Russia.

When he kicked his hat out of the tent. When it filled with snow.

The afternoon dragged on forever, made worse by a surprise math test. I couldn't concentrate on the questions, couldn't make sense of the fractions, the greater-thans.

At last the bell rang. Outside, a fresh layer of snow lay on the schoolyard. In my mind it became Russia. I saw broken tents and stumbling horses with wet manes and men sprawled face down and the snow stained red with their blood.

I got on my bike and pedaled hard, my tires making slush.

As I approached our house I saw a small green van pulling away from the curb, leaving tire tracks in the whiteness. Mr. Karp stood on the veranda without a jacket or hat, but he didn't see me and went inside.

I ditched my bike, went into the front hall, yanked off my boots and jacket and scarf and hat and mitts, and ran up the two flights of stairs, knocking loudly on the trap door.

"Mr. Karp! It's me, Randolph."

I waited. I waited some more.

At last the door opened and I climbed up to find Mr. Karp in his cardigan sweater, looking kindly at me.

"Ah, Randolph. Do come in. You must forgive me for being slow but I'm rather tired from such a long trip."

"We thought you were never coming back," I said, but then I stopped. I looked past Mr. Karp at the bare wall behind him and then I turned and looked at the whole room.

It was empty. No bed. No night table. No lamp.

"Mr. Karp, what's going on?" I asked, but before he had a chance to answer, I stepped into the other room.

No Persian rug. No three-legged table and chair. No shelves. And no containers.

Only a stack of wooden crates marked FRAGILE and PERISHABLE.

"I am moving out," Mr. Karp said quietly.

"You're moving out?" I repeated.

"Yes, I'm sorry to say. I was most comfortable here. And I have enjoyed our friendship, Randolph."

I didn't understand. Why would Mr. Karp move? Wasn't our third floor nice enough for him? But it was nice! Didn't he have enough room for his collection?

And then I remembered.

"The Nakajima Sample. Can I see it, Mr. Karp? Melted snow from Napoleon's hat! That's so amazing. I was reading about him in the library."

"I didn't get it, Randolph."

"What?"

I stared at him. He did look really tired.

The skin under his eyes sagged. His cheeks were gray.

"How come you didn't get it?" I asked in a small voice. "Did she decide not to sell it?"

"No, she sold it." Mr. Karp's eyebrow rose a little.

"Oh, no," I said. "Ravelson."

"Yes."

I couldn't believe it. It wasn't fair. It couldn't be.

"How?"

"R.B. Purcell."

"The Reliable Agent?"

"I'm afraid so. He was secretly working for Ravelson, too. Had been for months. Not exactly what you'd call good sportsmanship, is it?"

"But that's just terrible, Mr. Karp. Now Ravelson is way ahead of you. You'll never catch up to him. You'll stay the second-foremost collector in the northeast."

"Not even that, Randolph."

"What do you mean?"

"I'd better show you something. Look here."

Mr. Karp took two steps and laid his hand on top of a crate.

"You've packed your samples," I said.

He shook his head slightly. A cold feeling, like a chill, went through me. Then he lifted off the top of the crate, which had not been nailed down.

Coming forward, I could see the containers packed neatly with little foam inserts between them so that the glass of one would not crack against the glass of the next. But something looked wrong.

I peered in. Then I put my fingers around the stopper of one and pulled it off.

The container was empty.

So was the next and the next.

"Where are the samples, Mr. Karp? Where's Sarah Bernhardt's bathwater? Where's the Delaware River after George Washington's crossing? Where's the water from Jackie Robinson's drinking bottle?"

Mr. Karp looked almost embarrassed, as if he didn't want to tell me.

"Gone, Randolph, all gone." Then he pointed his finger at the sink.

"You poured them down the drain?"

He nodded.

"But why?"

"Because it was too much. Because I couldn't think of anything but my collection. I wanted to be the foremost collector in the northeast too badly. I had nothing else, no real life. So I've got rid of it all. It wasn't easy. It made me sick to do it. At one point — I'd poured about half of them out — I had to put my head out the window for fresh air. I thought I would faint. But they all went down, every last drop. And now I'm free, Randolph. Free after all these years. I've sold all my belongings."

"But what about your job?"

"I've quit. I'm no longer the complaints department of Macintosh's department store. But then who am I? That's the question. You know, it's a little scary to be free. But exciting, too. I'm going to travel. Instead of owning things, I'm going to see and do things. I don't know where I will go or who I will meet, but I know it will be an

FRAGILE
PERISHABLE
FRAGILE
FRAGILE
FRAGILE
FRAGILE

adventure. Do you understand, Randolph? I'm going to really live now."

I wasn't sure if I did understand.

Mr. Karp looked pale and his lips were trembling. He went over to the sink and placed his hands on the rim to steady himself. He turned on the tap and splashed water on his face.

After that he took a glass — there was just one on the shelf over the sink — filled it from the tap and quickly drank half of it down. Then he looked at me and smiled.

"You see that, Randolph? That's what water is for. Drinking. Washing. Swimming! I'm going to swim in rivers and lakes. I'm going to jump in waterfalls."

He put down the glass and held out his hand for me to shake.

"It was good knowing you, my young friend."

He got his coat and hat from a peg in the wall. He put them on and picked up his rubber overshoes. He went through the trap door and down the stairs and I followed him. At the front door he put on his overshoes and walked down the veranda stairs, leaving prints in the new snow.

A yellow cab waited at the curb. Mr. Karp slowly got into the back and the cab drove off down the street.

I remained at the door watching the snow fall until from somewhere inside my older sister shouted, "Are you trying to freeze me to death? Shut the door!"

In the front hall I saw a newly delivered copy of *The Drip*. I picked it up and pulled out the staple to unfold it.

There was a front-page photograph of Ravelson holding up the Nakajima Sample. You could see he was in Japan because of some temple behind him and signs in Japanese.

I stuck the paper in my back pocket and went up the stairs, pausing by my room for a moment and then continuing up.

I emerged through the trap door on to the third floor and went to the window and watched the snow.

I hadn't wanted a tenant on our third

floor, hadn't wanted Mr. Karp to come, and now I was sorry he was gone.

Turning around, I noticed Mr. Karp's glass by the sink, the one he had been drinking from. I picked up the glass and looked at the ordinary clear water, the way the water always looked in our town.

I went over to the pile of crates. Why, I wondered, hadn't Mr. Karp loaded them into the van, too? Maybe he was planning to come back for them, but it hadn't sounded like it.

From down below I heard my dad's voice.

"Randolph, where are you? I've got some ideas for the new hardware store sign. I need your opinion."

"I'll be there in a minute," I called back.

I lifted out the glass container that I'd looked at before, the one with the stopper pulled out.

It was dry inside and spotlessly clean. Even the little label was blank.

I picked up the glass and carefully poured the water into the container. I put the glass down and put the stopper back on the container, making sure it was tight. I fished around in my pocket and found a stub of pencil.

In clear letters I printed on the label:

Mr. Karp's Last Glass

Underneath, in smaller letters I added the date and the address of our house and the name of our town and our country.

Holding the container in both hands, I carried it to my room. I put it on my desk and looked at it for a long moment.

And then I ran out of the room and along the hall and down the stairs.

THE DRIP
YOUNG COLLECTOR MAKES WAVES
COLLECTOR